for Katie Randall and Virgil

with love

Also by Catherine Brighton

HOPE'S GIFT
THE VOICE : A SEQUENCE OF POEMS BY WALTER DE LA MARE
THE PICTURE
MARIA

Famous Childhoods
NIJINSKY
MOZART
FIVE SECRETS IN A BOX

First published in 1991
by Faber and Faber Limited
3 Queen Square London WCIN·3AU

Photoset by Input Typesetting Ltd London.

Printed in Belgium by
Proost International Book Production
Turnhout, Belgium

Text and illustrations © Catherine Brighton, 1991

Letters written by Frederick Marns

Catherine Brighton is hereby identified as author and illustrator
of this work in accordance with Section 77
of the Copyright, Designs and Patents Act 1988.

A CIP record for this book is available from the British Library

ISBN 0-571-14068-8

Dearest Grandmama

written and illustrated

by

Catherine Brighton

ff

faber and faber

1 November 1830   <u>Meralda</u>, at sea.

Dearest Grandmama,

 It is a whole year since I left. I do hope you received my letters from Africa and you liked my funny drawings. All these letters will be posted on to you when we reach our next landfall.

 Today I am tying labels on the shells that Papa has found. Down in the dark hold Papa keeps the creatures he has captured in big crates. Mr Tubbs, the ship's cook, lets me feed them if I am really careful. Mr Snaughty has cut my lovely hair! I know you will not mind because it is getting in the way when I go swimming. Yes, I can swim! well, nearly.

 Your loving grand—daughter,

 Maudie—Ann

7 November 1830   <u>Meralda</u>, at sea

Dearest Grandmama,

      This evening I went wandering along the ship's rail. I was looking over the side into the dark sea when I saw a boy climbing out of a small boat. He was climbing up on to the <u>Meralda</u>! The crew were too busy singing to hear my calling so I helped him up myself. He never said a word as I took him past the singing sailors and down to the cabins. Mr Tubbs gave me some food but the silent boy just pushed it away. What kind of boy is it, Grandmama, who comes from nowhere and does not eat or speak?

        Your loving grand-daughter
           Maudie-Ann

8 November 1830   <u>Meralda</u>, at sea

Dearest Grandmama,

I have found some clothes for the silent boy.

As I hung the boy's raggedy jacket on the door, Grandmama, a letter dropped out. I remember my dear departed Mama telling me not to read other people's letters but without thinking, I am afraid I read it, Grandmama.

It said:

"Dear Doctor Estepona,

This is the boy I spoke of in my last letter. I am sending him to you from the port of New York in the care of the Captain of the Marie Celeste.

As I explained he has not spoken for three years now and I have done all I can. I hope most sincerely that your new methods might help him.

Yours very sincerely,

Doctor Alban Bishop"

But Grandmama, the letter was dated 1872, <u>forty years into the future</u>!

When the silent boy was dressed I took him to Papa's mirror to show him how smart he looked. I stared and stared, Grandmama, but I could only see myself! He had <u>no reflection</u>! I got very angry and shook him and turned him round and still there was no reflection.

What kind of boy is it, Grandmama, who does not have a reflection?

Your loving grand-daughter,

Maudie-Ann

11 November 1830   <u>Meralda</u>, at sea

Dearest Grandmama,

      This morning I took the silent boy to Papa's laboratory where we keep the specimens. It smells of chemicals but he didn't mind. I showed him the stuffed birds that stare down from every shelf and the skeletons that rattle when the <u>Meralda</u> sways. But then he heard the ship's clock and he covered his ears and turned away. I closed the lid and because he still looked frightened I turned the tiny key.

      "Look," I said, "I've locked it. I have made time stand still."

      After that he smiled and we sat at Papa's desk and I showed him the shells. But what kind of boy is it, Grandmama, who is frightened of time?

      Your loving grand-daughter,

      Maudie-Ann

14 November 1830   <u>Meralda</u>, at sea

Dearest Grandmama,

We have had a bad storm and the <u>Meralda</u> has been tossed by huge waves. Papa was worried about the creatures in the hold because the crates were breaking up.

I hung on tight, Grandmama, as the sea rolled across the deck. I shall never forget what I saw when my eyes cleared. One of Papa's creatures, a thing he calls a 'crocodile', was coming towards me! As I ran to escape another wave swept me towards the edge of the ship. If the silent boy had not been there to grab me I would surely have drowned in the thundering waves. What kind of boy is it, Grandmama, who is not afraid of dying in the angry sea?

Your loving grand-daughter,

Maudie-Ann

20 November 1830   _Meralda_, at anchor

Dearest Grandmama,

The weather is very different now.

The sun is baking hot and every now and then a tiny breeze ruffles a sail. The _Meralda_ has passed into calmer waters and we are anchored amongst some small islands. When we look over the side the silent boy and I can see thousands of brightly coloured fish darting between the rocks. When I look at my reflection in the smooth surface of the sea I am alone. There is no reflection of the boy.

Papa has decided to explore the islands because there will be plants and creatures that he has never seen.

The crew lower the boats, we all climb in and row to the island. A tropical island, Grandmama, is not much like home. There are huge butterflies and monkeys that hide in the trees. They throw coconuts down and one hit the silent boy but, Grandmama, he did not even notice.

What kind of boy is it, Grandmama, who does not feel pain?

Your loving grand-daughter

Maudie-Ann

21 November 1830   <u>Meralda</u>, at anchor

Dearest Grandmama,

    While Papa was searching the island for specimens, the silent boy and I returned to the beach. We trailed our hands in the rock pools and watched the tiny fishes darting away. Under our feet the sand was littered with shells and I noticed the silent boy was collecting them and putting them in his pocket.

    The hot sun beat down on the sand as I fished for Blue Tangs and as I looked at the silent boy threading his shells, I realized that he did not have a shadow.

    Later in the afternoon, when we were climbing in the rigging, the silent boy gave me his string of shells to wear around my neck. As the sky turned from blue to purple and the sun was beginning to set I turned to the silent boy and said,

"Look, the sun is sinking!"

And then, Grandmama, the boy turned to me and <u>spoke</u>!

He repeated my word!

"Sinking! Sinking! Sinking!" But that was all he said.

What kind of boy is it Grandmama, who has only one word and that word is "Sinking"?

I have left the silent boy up in the rigging watching the sun setting.

Your loving grand-daughter

Maudie~Ann

<u>Dearest Grandmama,</u>

I am so sad I can hardly write.

The silent boy has gone. When I awoke this morning he was nowhere in sight. I ran up and down the deck calling. I thought he was hiding. The crew looked confused and called for Papa. He carried me, kicking and struggling, to his cabin.

"What is the matter, Maudie~Ann?" he asked I told him the silent boy had gone.

And then, Grandmama, do you know what Papa said?

He said, "What boy, Maudie~Ann? There was no boy."

"But, Papa! The silent boy! The boy with no shadow and no reflection! The boy who could feel no pain and only said "sinking"!"

I was crying, Grandmama.

"You must have imagined it," said Papa, and he made me lie down.

Oh, Grandmama, I did not just imagine him.

Your sad, sad, grand~daughter,

Maudie~Ann

4 December 1830

Hotel de los Vistas
Rio de Janeiro
Brazil

Dear Mother,

I am afraid Maudie~Ann has not been very well.

I think it is due to the heat. However I may not have paid her enough attention.

She became very upset the other day because she claimed she had a little friend from the future and he had disappeared! She says he came from a boat called the <u>Marie Celeste</u>. I even checked in the Registry of Ships to show her no such vessel exists.

I have taken Maudie~Ann shopping in Rio and saw some interesting sights. She seems much happier now and is looking forward to the next part of the voyage. I have sent her letters on to you and she will write again soon, but she asked me to tell you she has a charming string of shells

Your devoted son,

Edgar

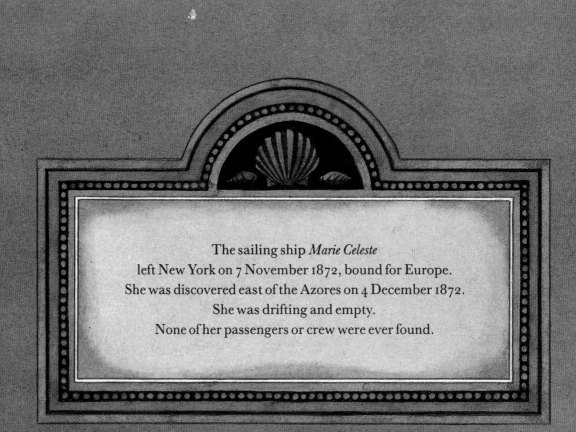

The sailing ship *Marie Celeste*
left New York on 7 November 1872, bound for Europe.
She was discovered east of the Azores on 4 December 1872.
She was drifting and empty.
None of her passengers or crew were ever found.